花 语 石 缘

詹 伟 的 陶 艺 世 界

Flowers and Stones
—— ZhanWei' s Ceramic World

前不久，我的学生詹伟致函让我给其出的画册写序，这不禁让我回想起当年他求学时的情景，那个在专业道路上孜孜不倦的他，如今，渐渐成长了，这让我很是欣慰。

詹伟是一个注重表述内心意象的年轻陶艺家，他的作品与众不同之处在于总是将视觉深入到作品物象之外，能引发观者对作品之外的联想。这次画册作品的效果和表达方式的多样性以及赋予的意义还是让我感受到一丝欣喜，能感受到这几年他在艺术探索上的努力。其作品涵盖了传统陶瓷装饰的形式，色釉的表现手法，瓷塑的造型风格，以及新的视觉样式和全新的艺术理念。在他的创作过程中，充分展现了自己独特的个性化层面，传达了他本人对于生活的一种精神体验，并且给这种精神体验以一种独特的表现理念，同时为学院派的陶艺带来了一种新的审美风尚。

我曾经讲过中国陶瓷的丰富多彩和优秀传统是中国陶瓷在世界艺术之林占有一席之地的重要原因，它所具有的鲜明的中国民族色彩、地域背景是全世界为之神往的。这其实就是"越是民族的，就越是世界的"原因。詹伟在学习西方的现代文化，理解西方现代艺术内在意义的同时，将自己的艺术之根牢牢扎在中国本土上，作品兼具民族性和世界性以及地域性与其自身的个性，这种创作的观点正是我希冀的。

近几年来，詹伟多次参加国内外陶艺文化交流，通过这些交流拓展了自身的视野，开拓了思维，这对其创作也有了更高的要求，我相信，他将在触摸火与土的媒介中，把"古今文化"与"中西文化"更好的融汇在一起，寻求新的方向，标示自我的个性，创造新的风格。

我想用松下幸之助的一段话以励其心志："人的一生，总是难免有浮沉。不会永远如旭日东升，也不会永远痛苦潦倒。反复地一浮一沉，对于一个人来说，正是磨练。因此，浮在上面的，不必骄傲；沉在底下的，更用不着悲观。必须以率直、谦虚的态度，乐观进取、向前迈进。"

是为序。

景德镇陶瓷学院名誉院长、教授

　　艺术世界的疆域是宽阔无垠的，它既展示着人与艺术之间的交往，又构筑两者之间延续的阶梯，同时也显示了人类生活中最感性的文化形式。作为接触泥与火的陶艺家来说，陶艺创造是一种创造性的活动，更是一种走向艺术世界的物质化艺术行为。

　　传统陶瓷艺术与当代陶艺的区别，造成了其同与异的临界点，我的创作正是基于这种临界点的实践探索，试图从某种意义上来创造出一种新的艺术图式，来表达个人的艺术情感并丰富着我们居于其中的艺术世界，使我们的审美生活朝着更为多元化的方向发展。这本画册的内容是多样的，但主旨却始终贯穿在中国本土文化样式上，诸如色彩、图式与造型，用的都是中国红、假山石、青花纹样、荷等中国元素。在创作的构思中，我把传统意蕴和现代构成形式进行糅合，通过中国的传统艺术元素来表现中国传统文化对当代审美的影响，把艺术形式和语言形态纳入到具象与非具象的形态对立中，使传统与现代互相融汇，营造一种具有东方本土语言特征的新图式。我也尝试在本体语言和艺术话语上寻求突破，本土特性的艺术特征和意象与他者艺术的冲撞和交融成为我构建作品内涵的重要表达方式。如画册中的作品《对影》以花鸟布局，构建了一个辽远空寂的画面，反映出随着岁月消逝对历史痕迹的留恋，作品以怀旧的韵味，配以中国红釉色装饰手法，将视野凝固在中国文化积淀中，试图寻求文明的印记。《宋人画意》则在关注中国传统花鸟画的基础上，借鉴了图式的视觉传达，从架上到架下，从平面到立体，构建了三维的艺术空间，以青釉向人们阐释了延展空间下的新宋代花鸟意境。

　　当代陶艺的发展，离不开吸收和借鉴，也离不开冲突和碰撞。这本画册中的作品只是我驾驭陶瓷媒介的一种尝试，有许多欠成熟和不完善的地方，期望观者批评指正。

　　最后，感谢我的导师秦锡麟先生给予我的鞭策和鼓励。

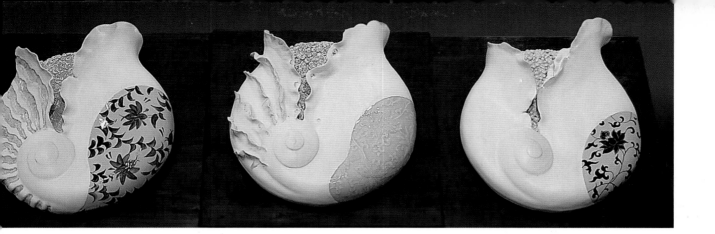

The boundaries of the art world are boundless. In the art world, people communicate with the art and continuously construct the relationship with it. Meanwhile, the art world represents the most emotional forms of culture in people's life. As for a ceramic artist who works with mud and fire all day, making pottery is not only a creative activity but also a materialized artistic action towards the art world.

The differences between traditional ceramic art and modern one result in breakthrough points. My work was indeed an exploration based on these breakthrough points. In a certain sense I made efforts to create a new art schemata, which expressed individual emotion towards the art and enriched the art world, thus making our aestheticization develop in diversified directions. Although the content of this album is various, its main idea is always related to the Chinese local culture and styles. For example, in terms of colors, patterns and shape, I used Chinese red, rockery stone, blue-and-white patterns, water lily, and other Chinese elements. In the process of my creative work, I blended the Chinese traditional culture and modern artistic forms and illustrated the effects of the Chinese traditional culture on modern aesthetics through using the Chinese traditional artistic elements. I also expressed artistic forms and language patterns via deliberately contrasting figurative forms with non-figurative ones. In doing so, I integrated tradition with modern and thus creating a new schema with oriental characteristics. I also sought a breakthrough in ontology language and art language. The confrontation and integration between the artistic features and images with native characteristics and other non-native arts became the major ways for me to construct the meanings of my work. For example the works 'Dui Ying' in the album depicts a peaceful and deserted scene in a layout of flowers and birds, which expresses a lingering impression of the past days. The work focuses on the Chinese culture and attempts to find the mark of civilization by creating a reminiscent mood in Chinese red glazed decoration. The works 'Song Ren Hua Yi' constructs a three-dimensional artistic image in green glazed decoration, based on the Chinese traditional flower and bird painting and referring to the visual expression of the patterns. The works illustrates a new meaning of Chinese traditional flower and bird painting in an extended space.

The development of contemporary ceramics will be handicapped if there is no assimilation and confrontation. This album represents my tryout in using porcelain as an artistic medium to express my emotions towards the art world. Therefore, there are unavoidably some inaccurate or immature artistic expressions. The advice from readers is always welcomed.

Finally, I want to show my thankfulness to my supervisor — Prof. Qin Xilin for his guidance and encouragement.

詹伟

　　江西婺源人，2004年毕业于景德镇陶瓷学院，师从中国工艺美术大师秦锡麟教授。主修现代陶艺与青花艺术，获文学硕士学位。现为景德镇陶瓷学院陶瓷艺术设计教研室副教授、江西省美术家协会会员。

主要展览及获奖：

2003年　第二届全国陶瓷艺术展览（唐山）

2003年　台湾第一届国际陶艺双年展（台北）

2006年　香港城市大学陶瓷艺术学术交流（香港）

2006年　第八届全国陶瓷艺术设计创新评比，获银奖、铜奖、优秀奖四项（宜兴）

2006年　第五届中国青年陶艺家作品双年展（杭州）

2006年　"蜕变&新生"——2007景德镇当代国际陶艺展（景德镇）

2007年　景德镇陶瓷学院赴中国美术馆展（北京）

2007年　景德镇陶瓷学院赴美学术交流展（美国）

2007年　上海艺术博览会当代陶瓷艺术家提名展（上海）

2007年　作品入选2007韩国第四届国际陶艺双年展并被收藏（韩国利川）

2008年　第八届日本美浓国际陶艺展（日本）

2008年　第五届江西省青年美术展览，银奖 铜奖（南昌）

2008年　第六届中国青年陶艺家作品双年展（杭州）

2008年　上海艺术博览会景德镇陶瓷学院教师作品展（上海）

2008年　隐藏的和谐——当代陶艺家邀请展（成都）

2008年　江西省青年艺术设计双年展 银奖 铜奖 (南昌)

2009年　赴法国联合国教科文组织中国景德镇陶瓷艺术作品展（法国巴黎）

2009年　建国六十周年景德镇陶瓷艺术作品巡回展（景德镇 台北 北京）

2009年　"景德大成杯"全国青花玲珑及青花日用陶瓷创新设计大赛银奖（景德镇）

2009年　上海艺术博览会陶瓷艺术展（上海）

2009年　第十三届江西省美术展览艺术类铜奖、设计类铜奖（南昌）

2009年　辉煌60年·迎新春美术作品展，特别铜奖（景德镇）

Zhan Wei

(1974-, born in Wuyuan, Jiangxi Province) majored in modern ceramic art & blue-and-white pattern design, under the supervision of Prof. Qin Xilin (The Chinese arts and crafts master) in Jingdezhen Ceramic Institute. He obtained Master Degree of Art in 2004 and now is a associate professor in the Department of Ceramic Art Design, Jingdezhen Ceramic Institute and a member of the Art Association of Jiangxi Province.

Major awards and art exhibitions:

2003 The 2nd National Ceramic Art Exhibition (Tangshan)

2003 The 1st Taiwan International Ceramic Biennial Exhibition (Taibei, Taiwan)

2006 Academic exchange of ceramic art in The City University of Hong Kong (Hong Kong)

2006 Silver, bronze and excellent awards, The 8th Competition of National Ceramic Art Innovative Design (Yixing)

2006 The 5th Ceramic Biennial Exhibition by Chinese Young Artists (Hangzhou)

2006 "Transformation & Renaissance" -2007 Jingdezhen Contemporary Ceramic Art Exhibition (Jingdezhen)

2007 The Ceramic Art Exhibition by Jingdezhen Ceramic Institute at China's National Museum of Fine Arts (Beijing)

2007 The Ceramic Art Exhibition by Jingdezhen Ceramic Institute in USA (USA)

2007 The Ceramic Art Nominated Exhibition by Contemporary Artists at Shanghai Art Fair (Shanghai)

2007 The 4th World Ceramic Biennial Exhibition 2007 Korea (Icheon, Korea)

2008 The 8th International Ceramic Competition MINO, Japan (Japan)

2008 Silver and bronze awards, The 5th Art Exhibition by Young Artists in Jiangxi Province (Nanchang)

2008 The 6th Ceramic Biennial Exhibition by the Chinese Young Ceramic Artists (Hangzhou)

2008 The Ceramic Art Exhibition by the Teachers from Jingdezhen Ceramic Institute at Shanghai Art Fair (Shanghai)

2008 "Hidden harmony" -The Invited Exhibition by Contemporary Ceramic Artists (Chengdu)

2008 Silver and bronze awards, The Biennial Exhibition of Art Design by the Young Artists in Jiangxi Province (Nanchang)

2009 The Chinese Jingdezhen Ceramic Art Exhibition at UNESCO (Paris, France)

2009 The Jingdezhen Roving Ceramic Art Exhibition in memory of the sixtieth national anniversary (Jingdezhen, Taibei, Beijing)

2009 Silver award, "Jingde Dacheng Cup" National Competition of Innovative Design of Blue-and-white and Rice-pattern Decorated Household China (Jingdezhen)

2009 The Ceramic Art Exhibition at Shanghai Art Fair 2009 (Shanghai)

2009 Bronze award in art and designing, The 13th Art Exhibition in Jiangxi Province (Nanchang)

2009 Special bronze award, "Glorious sixty years" ·The Art Exhibition in Spring (Jingdezhen)

醉心红莲之二　Enchanting Red Lotus Flower II
瓷　1320℃　142cm×45cm

醉心红莲之一　Enchanting Red Lotus Flower I
瓷　1320℃　142cm×45cm

醉心红莲之三　Enchanting Red Lotus Flower III

瓷　1320℃　142cm×45cm

醉心红莲之四　Enchanting Red Lotus Flower IV

瓷　1320℃　142cm×45cm

醉心红莲（局部）
Enchanting Red Lotus Flower （Partial）

碧嶂尽晴空之二　Bright Mountains and Clear Skies II
瓷　1320 ℃　90cm×12cm×20cm

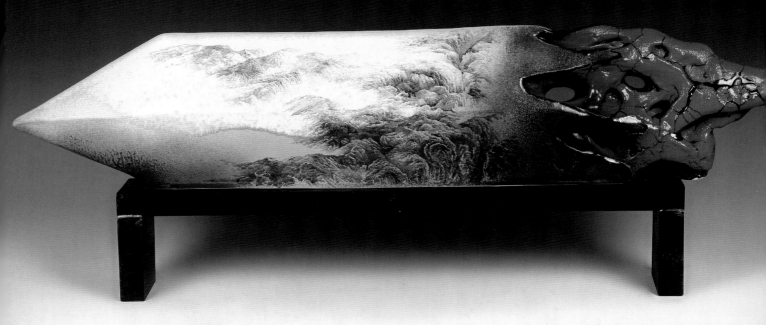

碧嶂尽晴空（局部）
Bright Mountains and Clear Skies（Partial）

对影之一
Shadows I
瓷
1320 ℃
110cm×23cm×15cm

对影之二
Shadows II
瓷
1320 ℃
110cm×23cm×15cm

绿影清荷　Limpid Lotus with Green Shadows
瓷　1320 ℃　75cm×75cm

落霞红妆　Sunset Clouds Crimsoned the Lotus
瓷　1320 ℃　75cm×75cm

鸢尾（反面）
Iris（Back）
1320 ℃
68cm×45cm×45cm

一脉幽香　Delicate Fragrance
瓷　1320 ℃　90cm×90cm

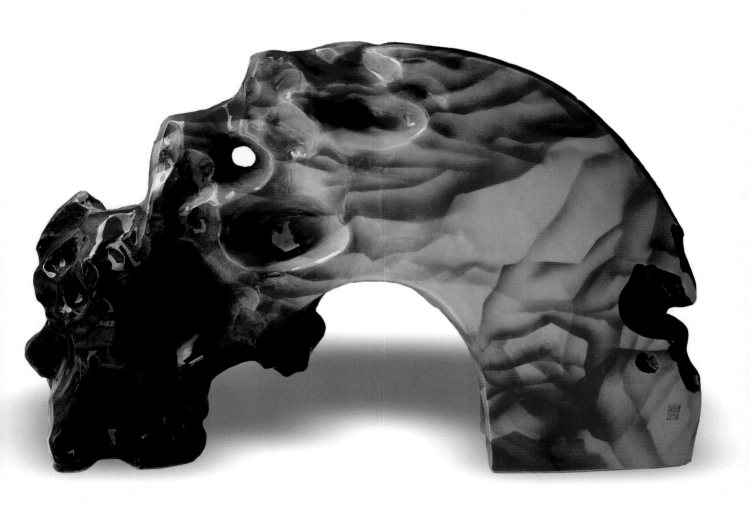

石之幻象
Mirage of 'Tai Lake' Stone
瓷
1320 ℃
65cm×56cm×26cm

飘逝的印记
Passed Mark
瓷
1320 ℃
110cm×23cm×15cm

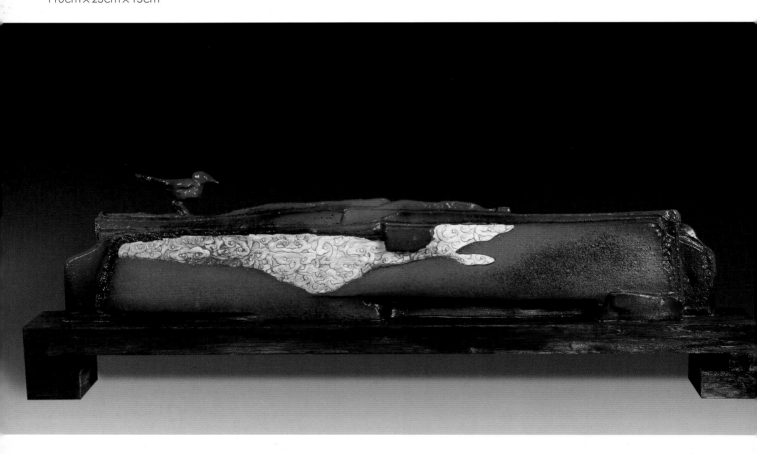

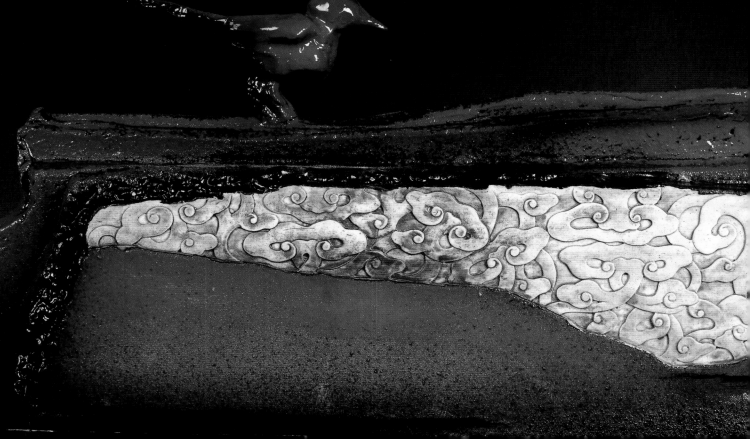

日照新妆（正面）
Sunshined Lotus（Front）
瓷
1320 ℃
60cm×35m×17cm

日照新妆（反面）
Sunshined Lotus（Back）
瓷
1320 ℃
60cm×35cm×17cm

图式新语
New Expression of 'sword'
瓷
1320 ℃
88cm×12cm×20cm

静思
Ponder Quietly
瓷
1320 ℃
43cm×55cm×21cm

宋人画意之一　Picturesque Scene of Flowers and Birds I

瓷　1320℃　42cm×19cm

宋人画意之二　瓷　1320℃　38cm×39cm　Picturesque Scene of Flowers and Birds II

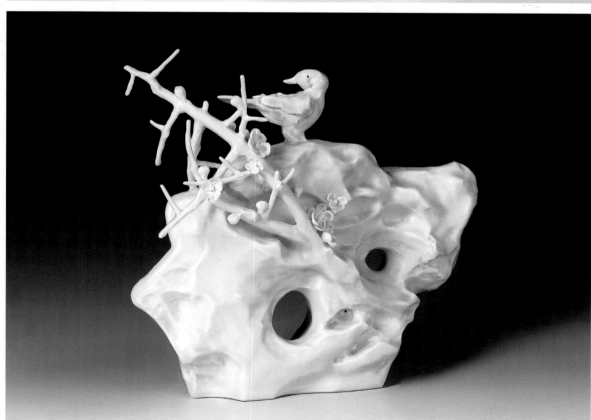

宋人画意之三　瓷　1320℃　41cm×39cm　Picturesque Scene of Flowers and Birds III

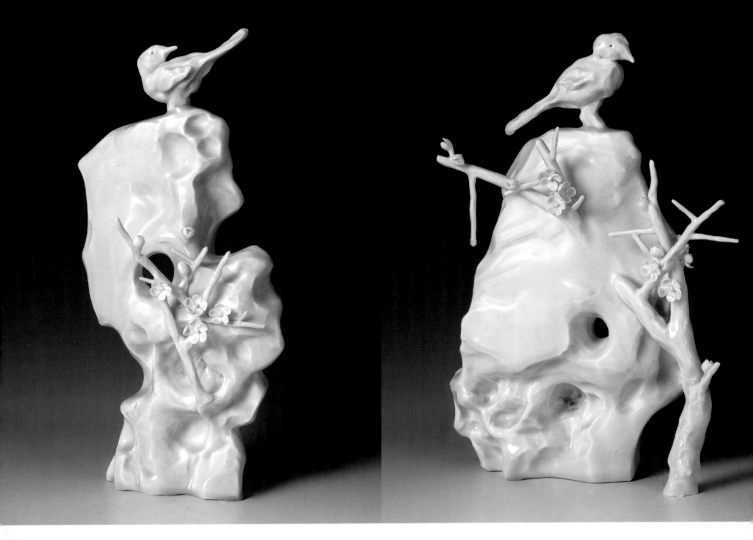

宋人画意之四
Picturesque Scene of Flowers and Birds IV
瓷
1320 ℃
35cm×30cm

宋人画意之五
Picturesque Scene of Flowers and Birds V
瓷
1320 ℃
40cm×38cm

宋人画意之六
Picturesque Scene of Flowers and Birds VI
瓷
1320 ℃
42cm×27cm

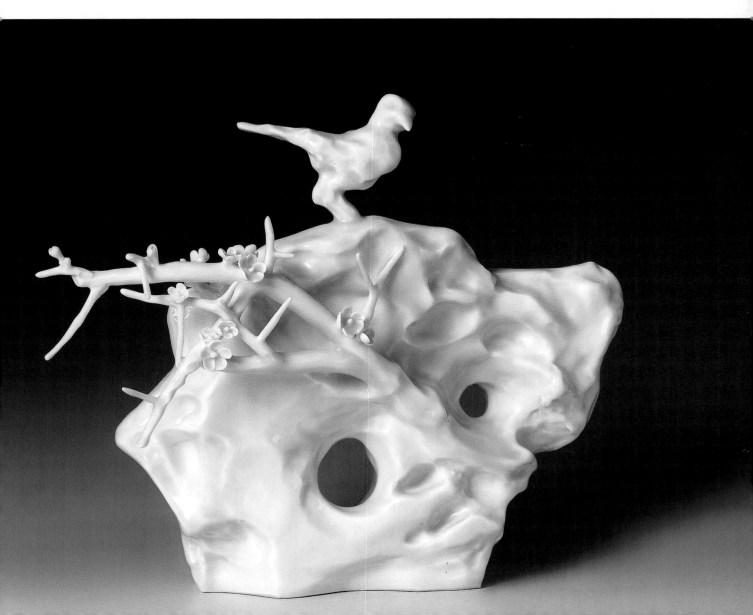

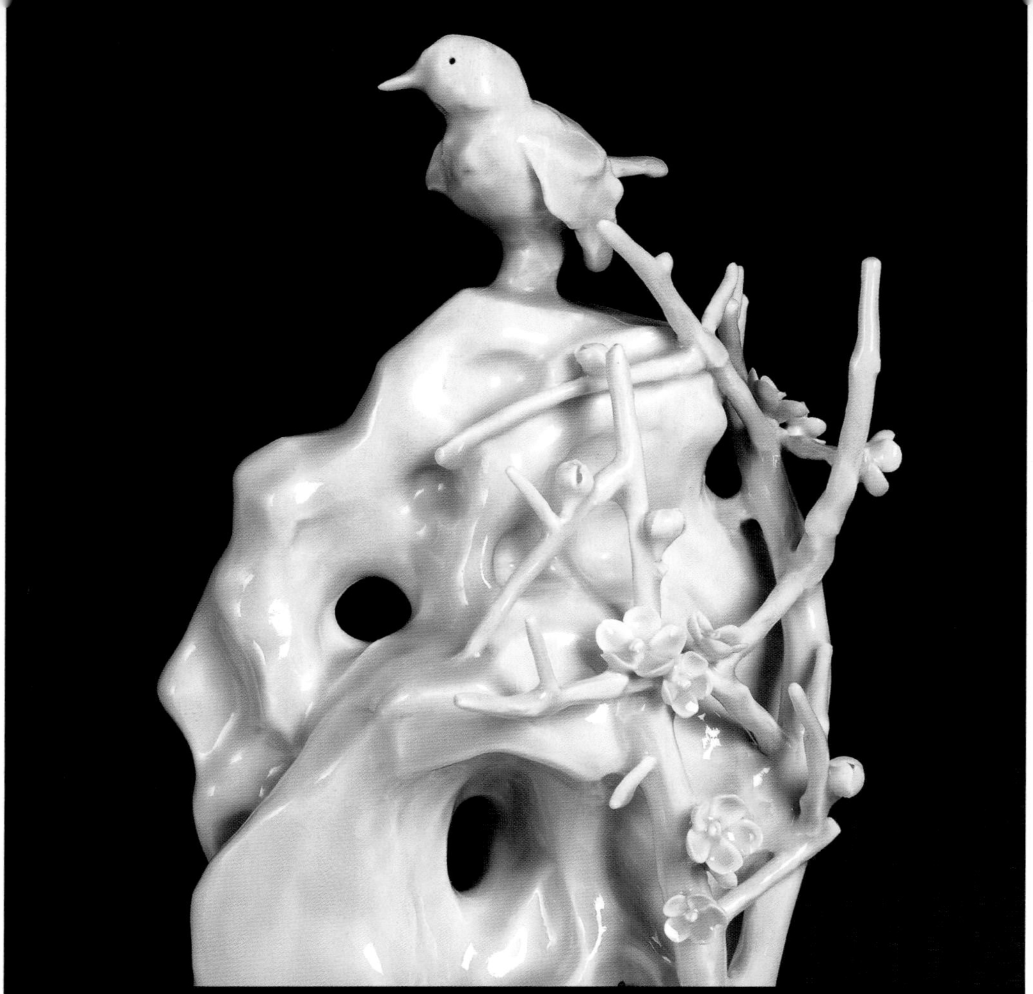

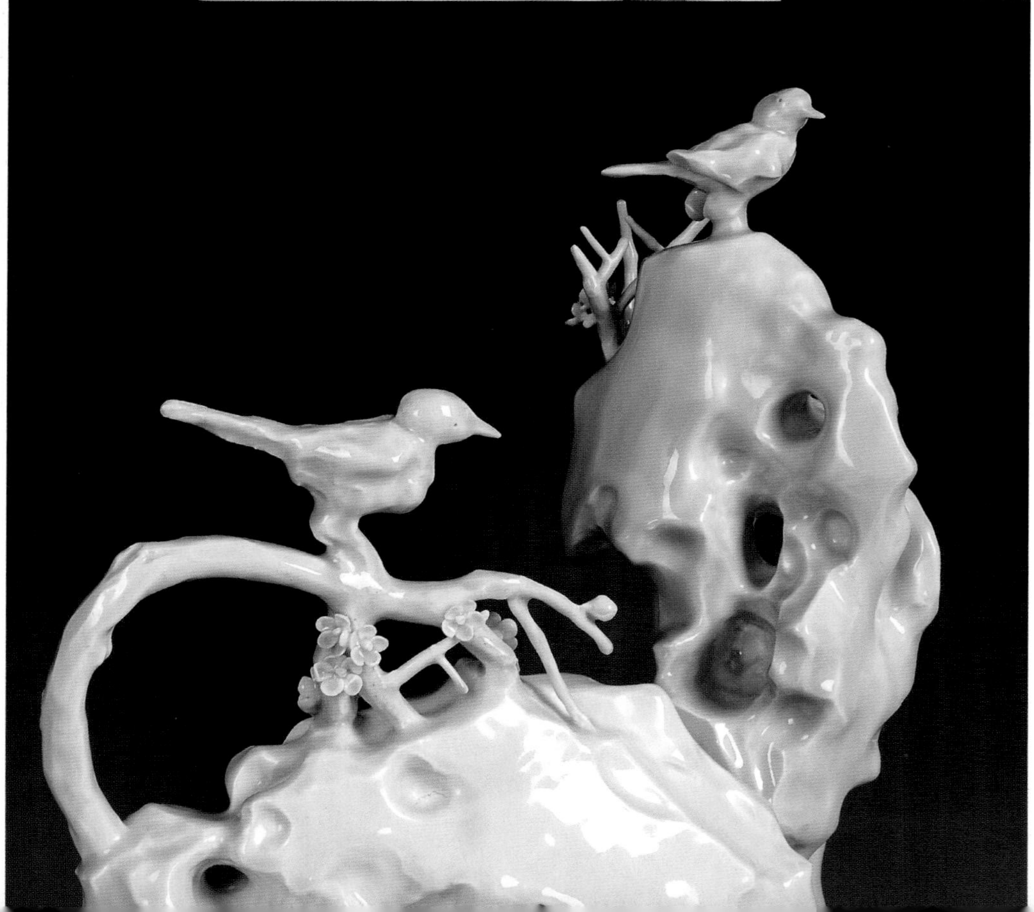

宋人画意（局部） Picturesque Scene of Flowers and Birds（Partial）

宋人画意（系列）
Picturesque Scene of Flowers and Birds （Series）
瓷
1320 ℃
40cm×38cm

青花之形之一　Shapes of Blue and White I
瓷　1320℃　45cm×35cm×28cm

青花之形之二　Shapes of Blue and White II
瓷　1320℃　46cm×38cm×27cm

古风
Ancient Customs
瓷
1320 ℃
58cm×30cm×21cm

一念之悟（恶）
Thought in a Moment （Evil）
瓷
1320 ℃
75cm×30cm

一念之悟（善）
Thought in a Moment（Good）
瓷
1320 ℃
75cm×30cm

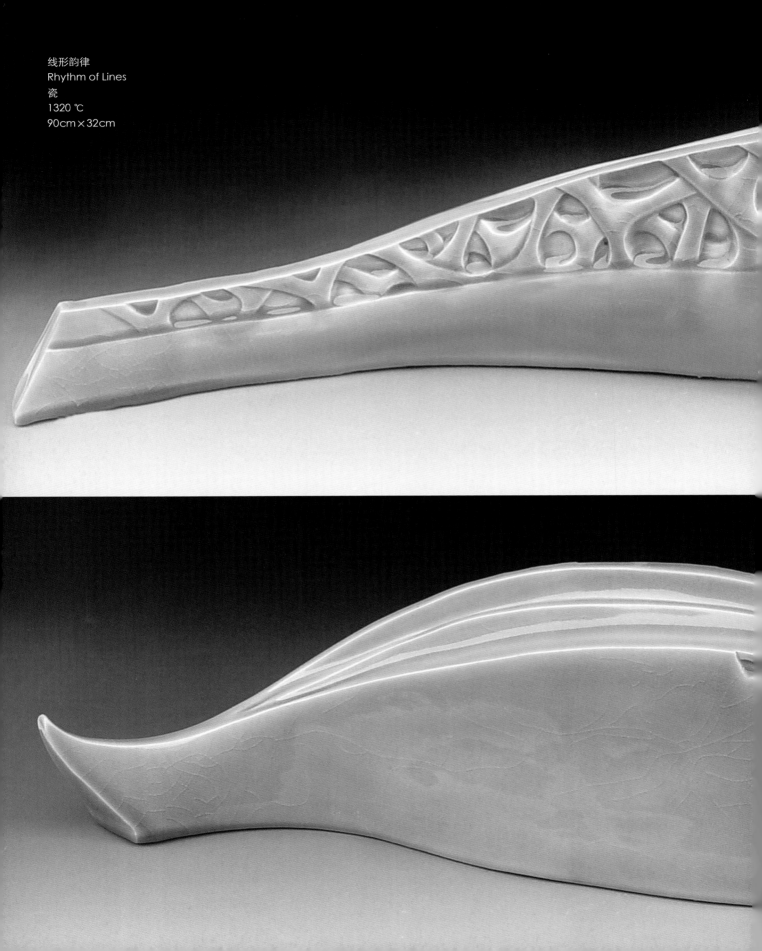

线形韵律
Rhythm of Lines
瓷
1320 ℃
90cm×32cm

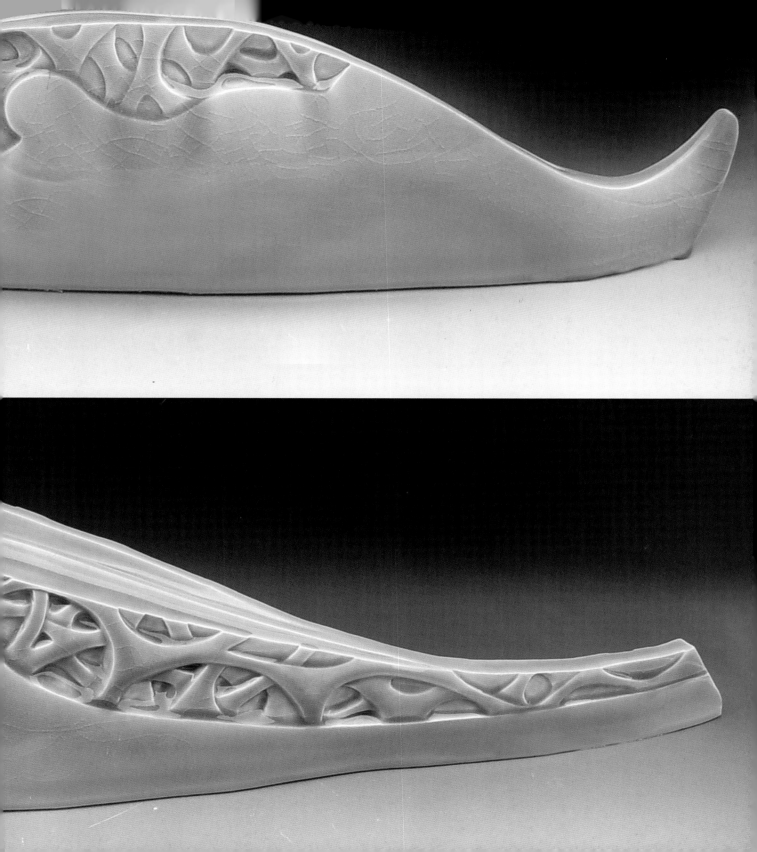

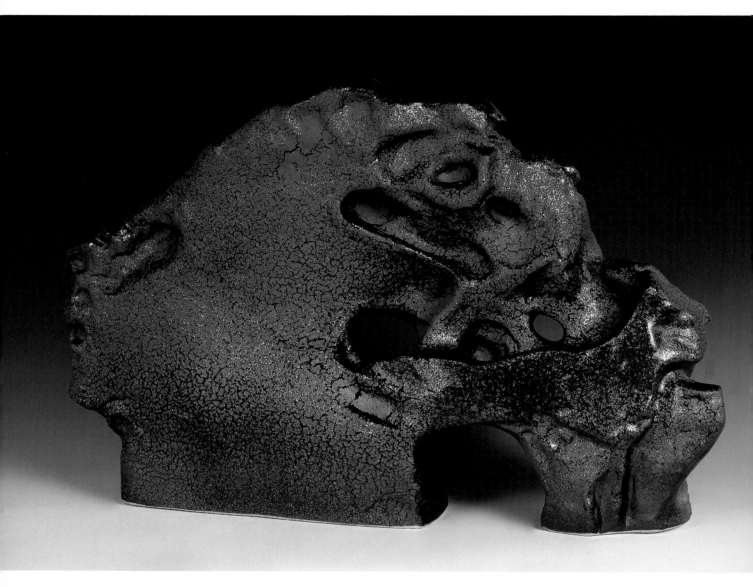

太湖印象之一（正面）
Impression of 'Tai Lake' Stone I (Front)
瓷
1320 ℃
65cm×56cm×24cm

太湖印象之一（反面）
Impression of 'Tai Lake' Stone I (Back)
瓷
1320 ℃
65cm×56cm×24cm

太湖印象之二（正面）
Impression of 'Tai Lake' Stone II（Front）
瓷
1320 ℃
65cm×56cm×24cm

太湖印象之二（反面）
Impression of 'Tai Lake' Stone II（Back）
瓷
1320 ℃
65cm×56cm×24cm

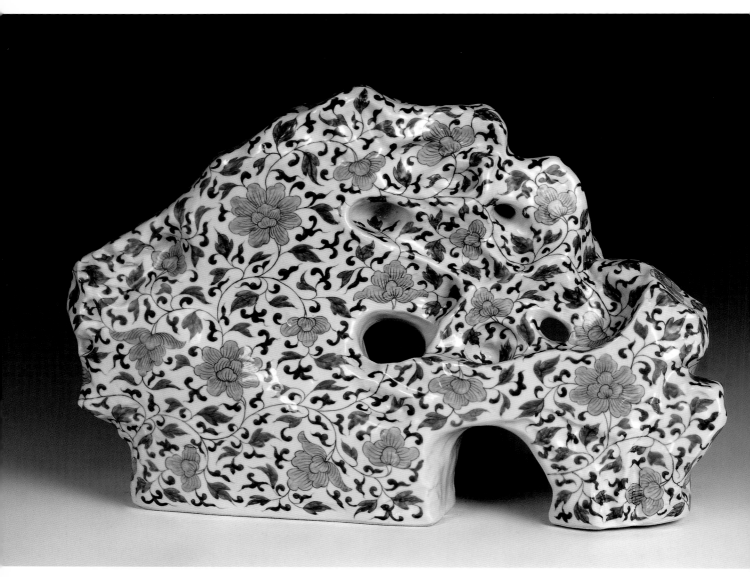

太湖印象之三（正面）
Impression of 'Tai Lake' Stone III（Front）
瓷
1320 ℃
65cm×56cm×24cm

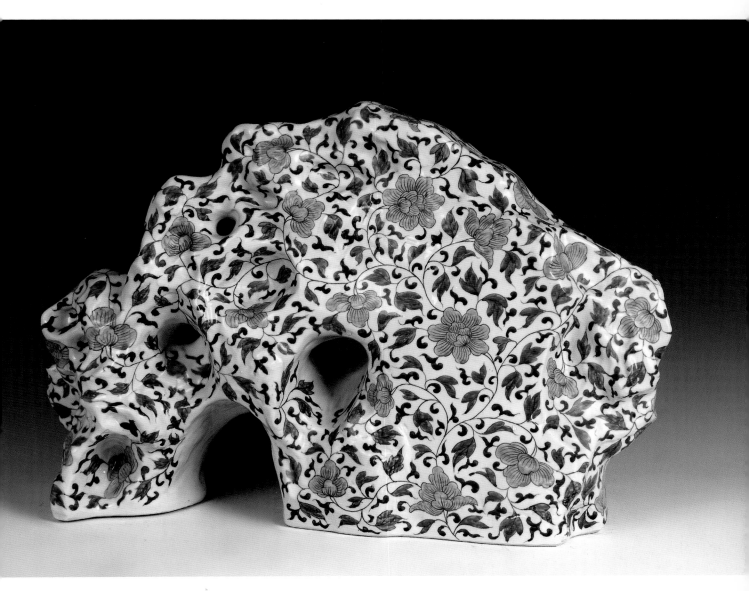

太湖印象之三（反面）
Impression of 'Tai Lake' Stone III（Back）
瓷
1320 ℃
65cm×56cm×24cm

图书在版编目（CIP）数据

深度追踪中国当代实力派陶艺家／李砚祖主编.－南昌：江西美术出版社，2010.11

　　ISBN 978－7－5480－0447－9

　　Ⅰ.①深… Ⅱ.①李… Ⅲ.①陶瓷－工艺美术－作品集－中国－现代 Ⅳ.①J527

中国版本图书馆CIP数据核字（2010）第204401号

深度追踪中国当代实力派陶艺家
SHENDU ZHUIZONG ZHONGGUO DANGDAI SHILIPAI TAOYIJIA

出版发行：江西美术出版社

地　　址：南昌市子安路66号

网　　址：www.jxfinearts.com

E － mail：jxms@jxpp.com

经　　销：新华书店

印　　刷：深圳市森广源实业发展有限公司

开　　本：889mm×1194mm　1/16

印　　张：15

版　　次：2010年11月第1版

印　　次：2010年11月第1次印刷

印　　数：5000

书　　号：ISBN 978－7－5480－0447－9

定　　价：120.00元（全套五本）

赣版权登字—06—2010—265